The Writer's Refuge

First published 2025 by Dahlia Books
ISBN 9781913624163

Copyright © Selection copyright © Northern Broadsides 2025

Copyright of each piece lies with individual authors © 2025

The moral right of the authors has been asserted.

All rights reserved. No part of this publication may be reproduced, stored in or introduced into a retrieval system, or transmitted, in any form, or by any means (electronic, mechanical, photocopying, recording or otherwise) without the prior written permission of the publisher. Any person who does any unauthorized act in relation to this publication may be liable to criminal prosecution and civil claims for damages.

Printed and bound in the UK.

This book is sold subject to the condition that it shall not, by way of trade or otherwise, be lent, re-sold, hired out, or otherwise circulated without the publisher's prior consent in any form of binding or cover other than that in which it is published and without a similar condition including this condition being imposed on the subsequent purchaser.

A CIP catalogue record for this book is
available from The British Library.

We gratefully acknowledge funding for this project from:

CONTENTS

About The Writer's Refuge ▪	1
Foreword ▪ Clare Shaw	2
Capturing Stories ▪ Shazia Bibi	5
Writers' Biographies	6
About Northern Broadsides	14
Our backs tell stories ▪ Hana	19
Meadows ▪ Anise	20
Pereybere Beach ▪ Stacy	22
The Last Minute ▪ Theja	24
What if I had a homeland ▪ Musa	25
Everything is gone ▪ Alaa	34
Questions ▪ Virginia	35
My Story ▪ Alaa	36
Hope ▪ Besara	43
An unknown ▪ Virginia	44

I am a river ▪ Hana	45
Expressions of the body ▪ Falone	46
Stigma ▪ Virginia	47
My Dearest ▪ Anise	48
He Dreamed ▪ Sofyane	51
Unbroken, unbound ▪ Sachal	53
My Story ▪ Anise	54
The lonely road was school to me ▪ Hana	58
Hope, Where are You? ▪ Besara	60
The six words story ▪ All the group	61
The Hill ▪ Theja	65
Reflections ▪ Alaa	67
Looking for ▪ Virginia	68
An adolescent love story ▪ Stacy	69
Memories ▪ Theja	71
The Most Beautiful Memories of Childhood ▪ Besara	73
The Distant Hills ▪ Alaa	75

A Mother ▪ Virginia	76
My Father ▪ Besara	77
Celestial Chains: A journey through the Temple of Dreams ▪ Sachal	78
Inertia ▪ Virginia	80
I was like a black ant on a black stone in a black night ▪ Falone	81
Dear Diary ▪ Besara	82
Poverty ▪ Alaa	83
What is Life? ▪ Besara	84
The global family ▪ Abu Rina	85
I am a Tiny Bee ▪ Theja	87
A home to the homeless ▪ Falone	88
The Writer's Refuge Allowed Me ▪ Anise	91
A Walk in Halifax with my Mother ▪ Basera	92
My name is not asylum seeker ▪ Abu Rina	94
End of a Happy Journey ▪ Theja	95

I am called happiness ▪ Hana	97
The goodness of the heart ▪ Falone	98
I'm here to stay ▪ Sachal	99
I Am Anise ▪ Anise	100
World in one centre ▪ Abu Rina	102
Hills ▪ Hana	103
Hope and Freedom ▪ Hana	104
Live With It ▪ Anise	105
When I Am Old ▪ Abu Rina	106

About The Writer's Refuge

Welcome to a collection of voices from around the world – poetry, letters, diary entries, and reflections which offer a glimpse into the diverse journeys of those who have been displaced. Their words stir emotion and provoke thought, encouraging us to reflect on how we lead our lives and support one another. These stories inspire and challenge you to live with more purpose and compassion.

This anthology of writings, created by refugees and asylum seekers, has been supported and facilitated by a dedicated team of allies – individuals who, though they do not have direct experience of asylum or displacement, are committed to justice and the importance of projects that amplify and document the voices of those whose stories must be heard.

The Writer's Refuge is a project by Northern Broadsides in collaboration with St Augustine's Centre, Arvon Foundation and Valley of Sanctuary.

Foreword
Clare Shaw, writer and facilitator

This is a very special book.

It took more than one person to write it. It took twelve extraordinary authors – Falone, Abu Rina, Musa, Anise, Alaa, Sachal, Hana, Sofyane, Stacy, Theja, Virginia, Besara. It took a group, it took a centre, it took a community. It took the whole world.

This is a global book.

In its pages you'll meet writers of all ages, of every gender and pronoun, from Cameroon, Sudan, Syria and Iran, Pakistan, Morocco, Sri Lanka, Mauritius, Nicaragua, Albania. You'll find poetry and stories, diaries and letters; departures and journeys; nightmares and dreams. You'll read about oppression, war and suffering – alongside courage, strength, and love.

This is a challenging book.

Like Warsan Shire said, "no one leaves home
    unless home is the mouth of a shark"
and this book reflects the range of painful stories that brought its writers to seek refuge. You should take care of yourself when you read.

This is an important book.

There are millions of people around the world who have been forced to seek safety and refuge far from home. More people will be forced to leave due to drought, flooding and other disasters, as well as loss of livelihood and insecure food supplies caused by climate change. Even more people will need to flee conflict, persecution and violence linked to climate change.

But this is still a hopeful book.

It was created in St Augustine's Community Centre in Halifax, in meetings of The Writer's Refuge – the friendliest and most supportive writing group I've ever been part of. It was written in the woods and by the river in beautiful Hebden Bridge, during a five-day residential. It was written in friendship. In his piece 'Global Family', Abu Rina describes how "everyone's barriers of fear melted away. Difference dissolved and our world became one family, a safe place for all."

I feel very lucky to have been part of this group and this book. As deadlines approached, I asked friends in the writing community to help us – and the whole community responded with offers of support. This is a book built of love, and community.

It is testimony to the skill and creativity of everyone who came to The Writer's Refuge. It is an expression of the courage and resilience of everyone who seeks refuge; and of the friendship, love and support we can offer each other. It is proof that we can all rise to extraordinarily difficult circumstances with extraordinary grace, beauty and kindness.

This is our book.

Capturing Stories
Shazia Bibi, Community Producer

Being involved in the creation of this anthology as a Community Producer has been a deeply meaningful experience. Documenting the work of writers – especially those from refugee and asylum-seeking backgrounds – is not just about capturing stories; it's about giving voice to those whose experiences are often displaced, silenced, or ignored. These writers are on a journey of navigating a complex path toward status, human rights, and safety after living through their traumas. It's crucial that their stories are shared, as a way of honouring their experiences, but also to ensure their resilience, hope, and agency are seen and heard.

Projects like this play a vital role in creating space for these voices. It is important to be committed to creating work that is both culturally sensitive and empowering. It is our collective responsibility to stand up for justice and equality. These writers' voices matter, and our job is to amplify them, ensuring they are the ones that shape the narrative. This book is the result of a team effort, but the most important voice is the one that is pressed onto the page – raw, real, and powerful.

Writers' Biographies

Falone Chapda Mougang

I am Falone Chapda Mougang, I am from Cameroon, Central Africa. My journey with writing was like a liberation from the stones and spears of my life. The beauty of words, the peace of the soul and joy of the heart. I felt love, I felt honesty, I felt consideration. I left Cameroon for England directly by plane after having some political problems. I joined The Writer's Refuge two months after I entered the country. I was so stressed and depressed, far from my family and friends. I am a young Cameroonian that was doing business and was also a hotel manager in my home country. But now in the UK, I am studying mental health and hopefully want to be a nurse in mental health. I just want to encourage everyone that is going through the asylum process and to tell them it's not easy but never to give up. There is better hope for the future and everything happens in life for a reason. Let us stand together for a better future of England.

Abu Rina

My name is Abu Rina, I am Sudanese, born in Western Sudan, El Fasher. I arrived in the UK in March 2024. I left the homeland that never left me for Libya after the war broke out in Sudan. I stayed there for months and then left for Italy by sea: there I sat contemplating when the road was lost in front of me. It was difficult because the people I met spoke little English, I sat alone thinking about the fate of this unknown immigrant (myself). I finally arrived in Britain, specifically the town of Halifax, and the lovely people there brought my life and spirit back again. I spent time in the company of inspiring poets, who made us forget the painful past for a while; they were truly a balm for a deep wound that would not heal except with them. At that time I realised how happy I was to see people like them listening to us with interest, to our pains, our tragedies. Now I am interested in treating the roots of the wounded past, so that the past does not cause the branches of the future to be poisoned, withered, and then die.

Musa Ganam
I am Musa Ganam from Syria.

Anise Pishgahi
Anise Pishgahi from Iran. I am an architect, but beyond my profession, I have always been drawn to creativity and expressing ideas through both design and words. Writing, for me, is a way to think more deeply, reflect on experiences, and connect with the world around me. I am also deeply interested in human rights and advocating for women, because I believe no society can truly progress without justice and equality. I am 35 years old and live in Leeds. My journey has always been intertwined with personal growth – whether through self-discovery, meditation, confidence, or self-worth. Along the way, I discovered Reiki – a form of energy healing that helps restore balance between body and mind. I have a deep interest in understanding light and awareness, always seeking to

explore inner truths and uncover the unseen dimensions of existence. To me, life is a continuous journey toward a deeper understanding of both myself and the world, and I constantly strive to walk this path with greater awareness and strength – not only for myself but also to help guide others toward clarity and enlightenment.

Alaa Al-Zuhaili

My name is Alaa Al-Zuhaili. I was born in a village in the Damascus countryside called Deir Attiya, located on the Qalamoun Mountains. I love my village and I love the city of Jasmine, Damascus. The writing journey began when I realized that all the words we say will not express what happened in our country. The writing journey was an expression of sadness and pain from the events that happened. I had many different experiences in Syria: at one stage there was a simple, quiet life, and at the other stage there was pain and suffering from the war. I decided to travel with my husband and children on a difficult journey of our lives. I collected the bags and inside them were pictures and memories. It was a dream trip and now we are here in the land of freedom in Britain. I say my word, smile, you are in Britain.

Sachal Envar

I am Sachal raised in the streets of a neighbourhood in Rawalpindi, Pakistan, where life is a symphony of survival – harsh, unrelenting, yet strangely poetic. Every alley is a story, its dust and shadows echoing the hopes and hardships of its people. In a world marked by poverty, crime, and drugs – where education was a privilege few could grasp – legends emerged from the very heart of despair. Souls turned their struggles into ink, etching their names into history. Among these storied voices stands my father, Envar Fitrat, a distinguished journalist and poet whose words carried the weight of truth and the depth of human experience. As I matured, my interests naturally broadened to include politics and journalism. Journalists reporting for PTI, along with workers and countless students, were arrested unlawfully and detained in underground prisons. I, too, found myself caught in the relentless tide of repression. In July 2024, with the threat of imminent arrest looming over me, I made the heart-wrenching decision to flee my homeland, carrying only my story as a beacon of hope amidst despair. My journey eventually led me to England, where, in the early days, panic, fear, and isolation became unwelcome companions. It was during this vulnerable time that I found solace in St. Augustine's, a charity in Halifax that supports asylum seekers with unwavering compassion and understanding – a lifeline that reminded me of the strength found in community. I carry forward the legacy of my father and all the voices who came before me, confident that even in the direst circumstances, art and truth possess the power to uplift, heal, and inspire.

Hana

My name is Hana and I'm currently living in Halifax (I call it Happyfax). I'm a single parent of a 9 year old princess. I'm from Pakistan. I'm a creative writer and a poet. I'm a survivor of modern day slavery and of domestic and sexual abuse. I'm involved in many community projects to give voice to many voiceless people. I'm a single disabled mother, I am an achiever, a dreamer. A freedom fighter, previously an asylum seeker and now a refugee. I joined The Writer's Refuge and I am glad I did. The experience was great. I made many friends through writing. And I learnt a lot. I am finally the story that I've been too afraid to write. The Writer's Refuge gave me confidence and allowed me to trust my ability to write and flutter my wings, and then allowed me to fly as the wings were mine and the sky belongs to no one. People put tiles over bullet holes and expect the bleeding to stop. It hurts every day, every time, every minute. It hurts. But joining The Writer's Refuge has helped me relive my journey of words with dignity and above all respect.

Sofyane

My name is Sofyane, and I'm from Morocco. The Writer's Refuge has been a great opportunity for me to explore my imagination and express myself through words in the most natural way. It has helped me overcome isolation and develop a new skill that provides mental relief whenever I need it.

Shelly Stacy Rebet

I am Shelly Stacy Rebet. I am from Mauritius. Being part of The Writer's Refuge has been for me an amazing and wonderful adventure. I have learnt a lot about myself through my writings and through the support of others in the group. Writing is a way for me to express difficult emotions and experiences. I am a musician, song writer, dancer and interpreter. Being part of The Writer's Refuge has given me inspiration to write again and have the aim to perform in the future. Whatever fear you have, it can be overcome with the right support and you can work on your passion and to have hope that all will be alright because you are not alone.

Theja Godakande Arachchi
I am Theja Godakande Arachchi from Sri Lanka. I was an NGO worker and a freelance journalist back in my country. I wrote and translated a few books for organisations that I worked for. From 2015 to 2021 I translated two books and wrote my own novel and published in Sri Lanka as my personal interest. I wrote a number of poems in my native language on Facebook and a few articles for some organisations in English. I received the invitation through St. Augustine's Centre. So I happily joined The Writer's Refuge programme and got a real privilege to know about Clare, Laurie, Valid and other amazing people. I am really lucky to know others who came from different backgrounds and generations.

Virginia Cerda
My name is Virginia Cerda, and I am a refugee from Nicaragua. I was forced to flee my homeland due to political and religious persecution. As a devoted Catholic, my faith

became a target in a country where religious beliefs like mine were met with oppression. My journey to safety was not easy. There were moments when I feared capture, times when I thought I would not make it. Yet, through it all, I felt blessed. With God's protection and guidance, I was able to escape unharmed. My faith carried me through the darkest times, and today I stand as a testament to resilience, hope, and the power of divine grace.

Besara Vishaj
I am Besara Vishaj, born in the village of Kolsh in the northern city of Kukes. I have a goal in my life which is to be grateful to God that I exist, to work towards being the best version of myself. Being content with life. My journey from my country to the UK has been terribly difficult. The five attempts - three times in the raft and two more on foot have been terribly difficult for me. God really wanted me to be here in the UK. The journey in this project has given me happiness because I have seen other people creating and realising their beautiful projects. I would define this part as admiration for me. This group brings energies of happiness when we are together. I have been inspired by those people who had reason to inspire me, and I hope to be an inspiration to, my mother who lives in Albania and my father who looks at me from the sky with what they have seen and experienced from me every day of life!

We all have illnesses, worries, fatigue, disappointments, but we have to be strong for every situation and now I have chosen every situation to just laugh!

About Northern Broadsides

Northern Broadsides is a theatre company based in Halifax, West Yorkshire. They create bold, accessible, and irreverent shows and inspiring creative engagement programmes.

They are well-known for producing classic and new plays that resonate with contemporary audiences while celebrating the cultural landscape and diverse voices of the North of England. For over 32 years, Northern Broadsides has toured extensively across the UK and internationally, bringing high-quality theatre to audiences everywhere.

As well as producing and touring their own shows, they are passionate about inspiring the next generation of theatre makers. Their Life in a Northern Town playwriting programme supports the creativity of young people across four corners of the North, develops work by new artists, and provides a ladder into the theatre industry for upcoming talent.

They also work very closely with the local community in Calderdale; running a free youth theatre in Park Ward, Halifax. The Writer's Refuge began in 2021, when Northern Broadsides began working with St Augustine's Centre in Halifax, to provide free writing, poetry and performance sessions for refugees and people seeking asylum in the local area.

Between 2023-2025, Northern Broadsides ran a community project for CultureDale (Calderdale's Year of Culture), Iron People. The project engages local people in a range of creative activities designed to explore environmental themes and connect participants to Calderdale's natural and historic landscapes.

Northern Broadsides Team
Laurie Sansom, Artistic Director & Joint CEO
Ruth Cooke, Executive Director & Joint CEO
Jess Rooney, Marketing and Communications Manager
Kassie Jones, Production and Administration Assistant
Sarah Oliver-Webb, Finance Administrator

The Writer's Refuge Team
Steph Connell, Senior Producer (Iron People)
Shazia Bibi, Community Producer, Park Ward
Clare Shaw, Writer and Facilitator

Board Members

Patsy Gilbert	Dan O'Gorman
Lucinda Harvey	Andy Pyke
Safoora Masood	Debbie Richards
Alicia McKenzie	Jesse Scott
Kate Mroczkowski	Leo Wan
Nelli Mooney	

Art Squad
Kash Arshad
Lucy Curtis
Daneka Etchells
Karl Falconer

Hana Gillani
Gobscure
Yolan Noszkay

St Augustine's Centre, Halifax
St Augustine's Centre is a vibrant community centre in Halifax, welcoming and supporting refugees and people seeking asylum. Working across Calderdale, they give people the practical support they need to rebuild their lives with dignity, and they offer a range of activities that help them feel happier and more connected.
Together they are building a diverse community which challenges injustice and puts the needs and voices of our centre members at the heart of our work.

Arvon Foundation
Arvon is a charity which runs creative writing courses, events and retreats both in-person and online. "Something magical happens at an Arvon writers' house. You arrive, perhaps feeling a little shy, uncertain and hopeful. You leave amazed at the progress you have made, encouraged by a sense of fellowship, a shot of inspiration and the determination to keep writing."

Valley of Sanctuary

Calderdale Valley of Sanctuary, is a compassionate and inclusive charity dedicated to fostering a culture of hospitality and support for people seeking sanctuary in our community. With a commitment to providing a warm welcome to individuals seeking sanctuary from war and persecution, we are proud to be part of the City of Sanctuary movement.

Further Acknowledgments

Editors and proofreaders are:

Kim Moore	Vanessa Napolitano
Claire Collison	Debbi Birch
David Tait	Polly Thomas
Elizabeth Chadwick Pywell	Elvire Roberts
Bobbie Sparrow	Alison Faulkner
Ute Kelly	Yasmin Khatoon

St Augustine's Centre:
Sara Robinson
Eve Wagster
Donna Kelly

Funders and supporters:

The Writer's Refuge is a project by Northern Broadsides in collaboration with St Augustine's Centre, Arvon Foundation and Valley of Sanctuary.

The Writer's Refuge is supported by the Community Foundation for Calderdale's Community Grants for Climate Action Calderdale Fund and Arts Council England.

The Grasmere Residency was funded by Wordsworth Grasmere and Glenthorne Quaker Centre & Guest House.

The Hebden Bridge Residency was funded by Arvon Foundation, with travel supported by St Augustine's Centre.

1-to-1 mentoring was funded by Calderdale Valley of Sanctuary (The Wharfedale Foundation).

The Writer's Refuge is part of Northern Broadsides' Iron People project, which is part-funded by the UK Government through the UK Shared Prosperity Fund, as well as Calderdale Council, The Liz and Terry Bramall Foundation, Tracy Brabin Mayor of West Yorkshire's Safer Communities Fund, the West Yorkshire Combined Authority's Community Climate Grants programme, Arts Council England, National Lottery Community Foundation and Community Foundation for Calderdale.

Our backs tell stories
by Hana

No books
have the spine to carry.

We are our ancestors' journey,
their wounds within us are buried deep.

Our backs tell stories
no books have the spine to carry.

Meadows
by Anise

In the heart of a lush green meadow, where spring had just arrived, and chamomile flowers danced under the soft breeze, there lived a woman who rose with the sun every morning. Her face bore the marks of years of hard work, yet her eyes carried a light that never dimmed. She was like a river flowing from distant mountains, winding its way through fields of flowers and grass. The birds sang joyful songs, and every time she listened, a smile graced her lips.

This woman worked tirelessly every day, beneath the blue sky adorned with soft white clouds. Her hands might have been weary, but her heart was full of hope. She never complained about her exhaustion, for she knew that just like a river carving its path through rocks and boulders, life was a journey full of twists and turns, beautiful in its own way.

In the heart of that meadow, the woman was like a breeze that, with every step, planted seeds of hope in the earth. Every flower that bloomed under her touch told a story of resilience. The cool spring breeze accompanied her daily, gently brushing her hair like a faithful companion. She conversed with the sun, drawing new strength with every ray of light that shone down upon her. Even in moments of weariness, she was like a river that might pause for a moment, but always continues on with power and grace.

In the evenings, when the sun slowly disappeared beyond the horizon and the sky blushed with shades of pink and purple, the woman gazed at the river flowing beside the meadow. The river reflected her own journey: it carried away its burdens, yet remained ever alive and moving. The sound of the water's gentle rush was like a melody that brought peace to her heart.

Despite all the challenges, the woman remained hopeful. She knew that life, like spring, always offers a chance to bloom again. Each day she passed through difficulties, like a river moving toward the sea, drawing closer to her purpose. In her face was serenity, and in her heart, a steadfast determination. She, like the springtime nature around her, was reborn every day, leaving behind traces of hard work, joy, and hope with every step.

And so, the story of the woman, like the river that flowed unceasingly, continued in the lush green meadow under the blue sky, with the songs of birds and the scent of chamomile flowers, forever in motion.

Pereybere Beach
by Stacy

To the north of Mauritius is a beautiful place - Pereybere Beach, just forty minutes from my home.

I love this beach. The sea is clear, and when you swim, you don't feel any rock or weed. You feel the soft sand under your feet.

I like going with my family. We search for a place under the Filao trees to sit in the shade. The sun is too bright – you will get very hot if you sit in it.

The kids get changed as soon they get there and jump in the water. Some play with the sand and make castles.

Sounds of birds, dogs, a few people screaming when doing water sports - such a joy. People singing and dancing.

Then the family shares all our different traditional food like fried noodles, mash potatoes, barbecue chicken.

I remember this as if it was yesterday.

The last time I felt those sensations, it was in tears.

I was with my father. It was the first time that I would leave my country.

We enjoyed every second we had there on Pereybere Beach, and we said, "We will meet here again". He told me that if I miss him, I should touch the tattoo that we both share.

I will always remember this moment. That moment and this beach will stay with me forever.

The Last Minute
by Theja

My daughter's lovely eyes, hesitating in farewell before she leaves,
my son's handsome face, his heart-warming smile before I run to hug him,
the final few stitches of my embroidery before I finish,
the colourful sky before the sun sets and vanishes,
the last few steps before I complete the hike,
the first glimpse of my friend, as my heart fills with happiness.
Everything is touching, soothing and exciting at the last Minute except only one thing, our happy moment on that day binds us with calm chatter,
love lives among us, that we never express through a letter,
but which floods our hearts and eyes,
gives us feathers, lifts us to the skies,
the instant I hate to remember, but can't forget, not ever:
the last minute you were with me, before leaving forever.

What if I had a homeland?
by Musa

My name is Musa. I am 20 years old. I come from a country that has lived through 12 years of war, occupation, destruction, hypocrisy, humiliation, rape and massacre.
I come from Syria.

Homeland is everything for me

The meaning of a homeland:
it believes in your principles
now and in the future

A homeland preserves your dignity and your personality,
your work and your studies,
your society and the people around you.

What if I had a homeland to protect me and take care of me? Would I have left for another country? – would this have happened to me if I had a homeland? A homeland that would give me the freedom and study I need?

My homeland does not preserve anything for me. There are no human rights. My homeland is terrifying. There is no security, no elections, no dignity, no work, no clean water, no food, no future at all.

Mountains

These mountains were terrifying.
Me and my brother
wondered how we could get through.

We used to climb the mountains every night and day
to cross to the other lands.

At night, we faced dangerous and ferocious animals –
bears, snakes, dogs, wolves. We could not sleep
in these mountains, we used to drink
dirty water, the water the animals drank.
We tried to filter it through our clothes
so that we could drink clean water.

Life in the mountains was difficult.
We lived there for 10 days without eating or drinking –
we were like dead people. No one knew anything
about us at all. The mountains are gigantic,
deadly frightening. People die
in the mountains -
nobody even knows their names.

A letter to my mother

Today I am writing a message to my mom. I haven't seen her since 2017. I haven't enjoyed it with her, I haven't said to her,

"good morning, Mom". I haven't kissed her hands, I haven't been with her on her birthday or Mother's Day. All I can say to her is,
"Be proud of your son, he is doing the best for you."
I love you so much Mom,
Musa.

Forests

There was a forest in Serbia.
In this forest, no one can escape.
In late afternoon this forest
would change to darkness.
So that we would not lose our friends,
we had to hold each other's hands.
We walked for two days without rest or sleep,
following orders, protecting each other from monsters.
But the border soldiers arrested us and started beating us.
They took off our clothes, they beat us
until blood came out
and they put us in a hole filled with filth
and cold, dirty water.
It is so cold, this forest.
Me and my brother put ourselves in bin bags
so we wouldn't die.

I am writing about abandoned houses

They were deserted, dark, damp, cold as snow,
no sun entering.
No people live there.
We used to sleep in abandoned houses
near the border.
When the border guards saw us, they attacked us.
They threatened us with guns.
They shot next to us to scare us.

Kidnapped

Human traffickers: those who trade in human beings; those who do not know the value of a person; those who take money in exchange for bringing human beings.

We were in Serbia, and from Serbia we went to Romania, where we were kidnapped by human traffickers. They kept over fifty of us in a house like a prison. They kept us in that house for 20 days. We could not go out or use our phones. They allowed us to eat only once a day.

Together, we fought with the human traffickers. We attacked them, we broke down the door and we ran out of that house. It was 3:00 AM and we found ourselves homeless. We went to the camp and the camp was closed. No one would help us. We lit a fire to keep ourselves warm.

After a few days we found other human traffickers who were even more dangerous than the first. They were carrying guns. They threatened us, beat us and robbed us. They left us on the road like garbage, close to the Romanian guard – who beat us and imprisoned us for three days.

We did not eat or drink. We slept on the floor in the prison and they left us outside around 5:00 AM.

I am writing about a dove

I was caring for it in my house. I was waiting for it to lay eggs. It brought me joy when I was a little boy, made me happy. I wish I could go back to the same age and live the same moments.

We used to wake up to these sounds in the forests. They were the sounds of birds like music. We felt peace and comfort.

Cars

We travelled by car. In Serbia, every night we tried to get to other cities, to Germany, Romania, five or six in a taxi.

The people were dangerous. They said that a van would come for us, but we waited outside for three days. We slept in the rain and snow and had no food, and nothing to drink. When the van came it was small; it could hold ten people, but they pushed more than twenty in. The driver squeezed everyone inside then pushed the door closed. We threw our all belongings away to make more space. My leg was breaking with the pressure, and we were all sick.

They packed us in like sheep, like animals. We drove like that all night between the mountains. The driver was drinking a lot, taking cocaine, driving fast away from the police.
When we arrived, we still had to pay. It takes weeks or months to travel through Europe this way.

In France, we tried to get inside a truck when the driver was asleep – we would open the big door at night, and someone would close it behind us. Other times, we would rip off the plastic and climb inside, and then someone would tape up the plastic. It is difficult and dangerous – if the driver sees you, he might take you back to another country. He might stab you, he might kill you. You never know what is going to happen.

Sea

We were at the top of the mountain when we saw the sea. We thought about how it would eat us, we would lose our friends and our future. It was the first time I saw this kind of sea. The waves were high and scary, making your body shiver. The sea was leaden and not blue. The weather was very cold.

Sea is treacherous. I asked my brother to go back.
It was unbelievable that we were going to cross that sea.

These seas eat everything. They eat your dreams. You lose everything you have in a second.

The sea is hungry. It wants to eat everything.

Boat

When we carried the boat to the sea the waves were high. It was lifting the boat up and down.

We were twenty people in a boat that could only hold ten. They put twenty people and a pregnant woman in a small boat and sent us into the sea.

It was my first time in the sea. I didn't know how to swim. It was like suicide.

The boat was heavy and water entered the engine. My brothers were looking into each other's eyes. We asked ourselves, is this the last journey? Will we never see our families again? The engine broke and the boat sank into the sea, and we were all in the water together. We were drowning like the boat, we survived with great difficulty.

Arrival

From the boat, the UK guard took us onto a massive ship. It was half an hour to Dover. My first sight of the UK was darkness, sky and sea and waves. It was so cold.

They drove me to a small station and took my fingerprints. I didn't know what was going to happen next. I was worried they were going to send me back. I had been on the boat for six hours. When I was sleeping that night, I felt like my body was still moving.

I felt like I was still at sea.

This is the journey in Europe

danger, fear,
     suicide, death

         If you want to give up you can
         give up no one cares.

This is what happens to a person when he is searching for a homeland to protect him, a homeland to prove he is not an animal.

I am 20 years old. I hope that when I finish my studies, I will get qualifications and open my own motor vehicle business.

Then I will travel to my wonderful family, and we will all sit together at the dinner table.

I wish I had the opportunities that my friends have so that I could study. My friends in England have many opportunities but they don't feel it.

We should know the value of things. We should know the important thing in this life – if somebody helps you, make sure you help him back. Life is like a wheel –everything comes back to you.

My name is Musa. I come from Syria.

Everything is gone
by Alaa

when I had life
oh full of life
my life was so amazing
without regrets

but now I have lost my life
oh joy of life
my world has turned against me
everything is gone

Questions
by Virginia

At what point
Did I become a movie drama?
At what point did chaos
transform me into a migrant?

Conclusions

I had to cross an ocean
to find a mirror
that reflects who I really am.
The forgotten

A small hand is stronger than two big hands.
Those who forget are likely to suffer again.
Those who stop playing no longer imagine.
Those who no longer fear the dark, fear living.

My Story
by Alaa

Our home street, the lights of our house. My heart trembled: I felt as if I was suffocating after I saw a picture of our street.

At that moment, the truth of the matter and the truth of the bitter war were confirmed.
The reality of migration and displacement. The fact that the country was empty of its inhabitants, ruined and destroyed.

My name is Al-Zuhaili. A Syrian girl, born in a quiet village called Deir Attia, on the tenth day of July 1989.

My life in Syria has become a thing of the past. But now I feel as if it happened yesterday. So many memories. My life is a train passing without stopping.

After my birth, my family moved to Damascus. We grew up there. We studied in her schools and grew up among her neighbourhoods. It was a happy life, though like many Syrians, we lacked many basic necessities.

No words can recreate my country, or bring back those times. There is no consolation I can offer to myself, my family, or my country. No poem or novel can describe the destruction and pain we feel.

My life is a train passing without stopping.

We moved between the countryside and the city; in the summer and holidays, we visited my beautiful village, which was about 90 km away from the capital. In the winter, we spent our days in Damascus.

My father and his brothers grew up as orphans after my grandfather was involved in the 1973 Libyan Arab Airlines Flight 114 plane incident, when the Israeli army struck a passenger flight from Libya to Syria.

Due to a technical malfunction, the captain had been forced to land in Egypt. Not long after the journey was resumed, the Israeli army attacked it, and it fell in the Sinai desert.

(One of my grandfather's old friends told me about this matter. He told me how my grandfather longed desperately to see his children. How he worked in construction so that he could secure his family's expenses in Syria. And what he did to obtain a plane ticket to come to Syria. But he did not make it home).

My father, like my grandfather, worked in construction. He lived a very harsh life – the loss of his father had a huge impact on his family. My father worked from the age of ten. He transported stones, and then he became a construction worker. Then he met my mother and married her... they had

6 children: 4 girls and 2 boys. I was the first child in the family... and then my brother Fahd, Walaa, Dania, Sham, then little Omar.

My life is a train passing without stopping.

It hurts to remember how my father used to go to work when the winter was harsh.
He said, "Whilst I'm alive, I want to give you as much love and tenderness as I can. I want to give you everything you need... I do not want you to lose the word father." Even as children, we knew he carried a great sense of loss, and he wanted to give us the tenderness that he was deprived of.

My father was perfect. Yes, he is my father, a piece of my heart. I remember how we went in the summer to pick cherries and apples from the trees in my beautiful village. Those were wonderful days. We had big dreams – they gradually faded as the years of war increased.

My life is a train passing without stopping.

I don't know what to tell you about the past. It is the season for picking olive trees, pomegranates, grapes, and apples, and also the smell of the wild thyme that comes from the valley, and all through my village, the smell of the lemon trees after rain. I will never forget those days, and my grandmother's house. On Friday, she would cook all the foods we loved, and she looked so happy. Now there is no homeland that unites us. We are scattered among countries. Each of us is in a place where we cannot see each other except from behind the mobile phone. We share our holidays and the birthdays of our children with our families only through the mobile phone.

I cannot describe the safety that my family surrounded me with during that beautiful period. But I can say... a person recovers with love, friends, and family; by laughing until they cry. The stories never end. And the warmth surrounding them, even on the coldest nights, is inexhaustible. A person recovers with the hands that hold them if they stumble. And the shoulder they can lean on if they fall. Yes. We recover with love, with support. We recover in good company.

We were all ambitious. I dreamed of achieving my goals – to turn my dreams into reality. I thought I was holding the paintbrush. I thought I was painting a beautiful picture. But before I finished, the colours all dried up.

The zero hour has struck. The war has begun. It is the fifteenth day of the third month in the year 2011. It is a volcano. It is the revolution of the people. It is the will to survive.

Is this a dream – or a bitter reality???
At first, there were only a few cries in the streets to tell the oppressor to leave.

It ended with the displacement of millions of people. Yes, Assad destroyed his land and his people for the sake of power. Thousands of young men, children, and women disappeared into detention centres, for saying, "No to injustice".

The biggest tragedy for me and my family in 2013 was the disappearance of my brother. My brother, who was a friend to me, and a part of my soul. He disappeared and we did not find him. We searched a lot and a lot, too. My cousin, we lost him with my brother. He was only 21 years old. Security arrested him like all the thousands who died in this damned war.

My last words to him were about bread and cheese. We were living under siege and we knew our father would not be able to provide us with bread so I told him, "We have to eat less bread". I did not know that this was the last phrase that would pass between us. He had gone and I knew that he would not return.

My life is a train passing without stopping.

Wars have no religion, and neither do the politics of states. These Arab presidents were not chosen by the people. They installed themselves, and we must remain silent, otherwise they will accuse us of treason.

The war in Syria continues, in instability and division. They divided my country into parts. Each part was taken by a certain authority. The Turkish, Russian, American, Iranian, and Israeli occupation in our country, and there is no place for the Syrians.

My dream was to escape from this reality. I decided we had to travel, however difficult or easy the journey was. There was no way to stay, no way back. The cruelty of the days drove me to it.

My life is a train passing without stopping.

Was it safer to risk my children in the sea? Yes. Yes, we had to leave so we can start living.

I decided to leave my country. I carried the suitcase with me. (Do you know what is inside it?) Yes, it is some memories, some pictures, and a lot of pain.

"The unknown prison", "the red prison", or "the prison beyond the sun" – that's what we called it. Sednaya. We knew that whoever entered it would not come out, but still we hoped.

When Assad fell, there was joy, and hope for a proud, free Syria. And we hoped to find our loved ones in the prisons. Instead, we found brutal torture.

Some bodies were fed to animals, some organs were traded. Bodies were transported in large trucks to mass graves. There was no space left to bury the detainees, so they used a press to compress the bodies and then put them into an acid pit. Others lay where they died, forgotten in solitary rooms. I don't know what they did with my brother's body.

My life is a train passing without stopping.

The shock is indescribable.

I want these people to be seen. I want to tell you about my brother, my cousin, my husband's brother-in-law, and our friends. I want the world to understand the suffering of ordinary people. I want the world to understand what this brutal regime has done to us. I want the world to understand how dangerous these people are.

I want us to build more schools than prisons and buy more wheat seeds than weapons. One day the sun will shine in our hearts.

Hope
by Besara

I had so much hope — I had everything.
Now my hope has narrowed
and I have nothing left.

Why did you leave me, O Hope?
I often woke you from sleep —
Did I annoy you?
I'm sorry, O Hope, for this —
but when I relied on you
I forgot all my worries.

What can I tell you?
You are a treasure, a true angel.
You are a light,
a candle in the darkness.

An unknown
by Virginia

I am a shadow of regrets.
The dove was swallowed by the hawk.
The girl who cries every afternoon on the wall.
The exile who begs for freedom.
I yearn to enter the place of my nightmares,
I drown my cries between words.
I am a wounded woman,
a wandering soul, a foreigner,
a Hispanic speaker. An unknown.

I am a river
by Hana

I have no identity
I am free and proud,
I am strong,
Once happy but now sad.
I used to smell like flowers,
Now I smell like poison gas.
Fish used to be careless and free, now they struggle to breathe.

Please, I need my friends,
Who used to keep me clean.
I need people to understand my pain which is very deep.
The thirsty tide ran inland,
And the salt waves drank from Me
And I, who was as fresh as the rainfall once...
But now, I am bitter and filthy.

میرے دوست اکہاں ہو تم ؟
، مجھے تمہاری امید تلاش ہے
اے دوست؟ اے دوست کہاں ہو تم ,کہاں ہو تم ------------

I need my friends who used to keep me happy and clean,
Where are you?
I need you, my friends.
I need you.

Expression of the body
by Falone

from my mouth to your eyes
from my heart to your soul
from my body to your spirit
from closed eyes looking far away
from my dead body wanting to rise again
from my blood to your hands
looking for a way to escape
from my legs to your destination
moving forwards for a better life
from my thoughts to your thinking
making life better for you and me
from my creation to your imagination
building a way for broken hearts
from you to me for a colourful future

Stigma
by Virginia

My whole life has been a stigma.
From my origin to my name,
from my roots to my dreams,
from my race to my beliefs.

From the most abominable part of my blood.
I walk naked, or I go covered in shame,
malnourished with love and
banished from inheritance.

That's how Eve must have felt
when she was expelled from the garden.
Who cut the fruit?
Did he ask for forgiveness, did he accept the blame?

Tell me Lord,
why among so many stigmas
you gave me one I never knew?

My Dearest
by Anise

Being without desire is a great pain.
It's like walking on the edge of an abyss.
Longing for you is the cure.

When longing and distance strike,
they plant the seeds of desire
deep in the soil of the heart.

A seed that cracks through its shell
grows taller with every second
and spreads its branches wide.

So wide that its shadow darkens
the heart.
The coolness and darkness of longing.

Imagination is the wings of desire,
the shortcut to reunion.
Imagined union is better than union itself.

Union happens once and ends.
But imagination repeats. Every hour,
every minute, every second.

Imagination has no end.

The world of imagination is mine.
I am its god and its servant.

I am my own sovereign.
I command myself to stroll
under the moonlight and the sun.

I command myself to kiss.
I command myself to quarrel and reconcile.
We are soldiers of this world.

Our weapons are longing and imagination.
We carry them delicately
and our bullets are this delicacy.

The world outside of imagination is coarse.
Its sun burns too hot, its trees give no shade,
its apricots are unripe. Its mint has no scent.

Its bees don't know how to make honey;
they only sting. There, even the lines of your face
are tangled and unclear.
But in imagination, everything is cool
beneath the shade of the tree.
The sunlight paints the patterns

of palm branches on your face,
clear and close. You are the shadow

of everything. And the faces of others

are all your face.

He Dreamed
by Sofyane

He dreamed of love, of family, of friends
gathering close, where the hurt could end.
A flash of light, a fleeting gleam,
a world where peace wasn't just a dream.

He vowed to fight, to sacrifice,
to spread acceptance, to pay the price.
To laugh one day, at last feel free,
to leave behind fear's dark decree.

He dreamed of a hand, loving and kind,
pulling him out and letting him shine.
A tiny spark, a peaceful sight,
but reality struck, cold at night.

Dreams turned to nightmares, hope grew old,
loneliness crept in, bitter and cold.
Speaking the truth brought only tears,
a voice that was silenced by shame and fears.

He left it all to feel halfway fine –
his friends, his family, all he'd called "mine".
Through unknown lands his footsteps led,
away from dreams and hands he fled.

Yet hope still glimmered, faint but bright,
a guiding star in the longest night.
Where the past was gone, a new life began,
where hearts are free, where dreams expand.

He walks ahead, with strength in his heart,
toward the dream he has carried so far.

Unbroken, unbound
by Sachal

I'm on a journey as a small spring.
As I left the shelter

of my guardian's wings,
I began to flow like a river.

Destroying the bustling streets
of greed and lies and betrayal.

I crossed the bridges of hope.
I followed paths of passion and courage,

I passed through stormy waves.
My journey is long, I face thunders.

The waves cry
and their pain is unheard.

The dark nights whisper.
Oh, this long journey, this river!

Yet in the depths, the king survives
and I am rising with the tides

unbroken, unbound.

My Story
by Anise

I am Anise Pishgahi, a girl from Iran. I was born in an educated and large family. Because I was the last child, my role models were four older sisters and three older brothers.

I don't know where to start, but I do know that I want to tell you the reason for my migration and the path of my migration that brought me here, with all its ups and downs, hardships, memories and bad events.

In Islamic society, girls reach the age of duty at the age of nine - and boys at fifteen - meaning they must fulfil their religious duties from these ages.

I always had a problem with these religious duties in my family. We were not a very religious family, but my father wanted me to learn my duties. I was a child and I did not like to pray and fast. I liked to play and be a child.

And I always had a problem with these religious beliefs. I was a child and did not like to go to Mass and sit still on the bench whilst the priest led us in prayer. I liked to play and be a child.

My story started when I was a teenager and started to not accept religion at all. I didn't accept the hijab and I wanted to be free.

As I grew older, my opposition to prayer and fasting and to mandatory hijab increased. I started researching religions and God. I read books and articles and the more I researched and the more I saw the problems of women in Iranian society, the more I realized my feminine power and wanted to change the world of women in Iran. I started with myself.

I was accepted by a university in a city far from Isfahan, I lived alone and became independent and more fully my own person.

During that time, I got to know women's support groups and my mind became more open day by day. I became even more interested in women's rights.

I wanted the women of my country to be free like the women in the rest of the world. I wanted girls of the next generations not to have the problems that I went through. I wanted teenage girls not to be ashamed of protruding breasts or their periods, which are a natural phenomenon of the body.

These convictions guided me and as I grew older and entered society, I became even more aware of the problems of women, girls and children and the branches and leaves of my mind formed and grew with the aim of supporting them.

As time passed, I became more and more aware of the government's oppression of people, especially women.

My family was opposed to my thoughts and actions against religion. They were afraid that if I did something, it would not end well because we lived in the Islamic Republic. But with the knowledge I had from all my research, I felt purposeful and determined.

In those days I was looking for a free life, the freedom to choose religion and optional hijab.

Little by little, through one of my friends who was a Christian, I got to know more about the Christian religion. I secretly thought of changing my religion from Islam to Christianity.

With the passage of time and the increase of economic pressure in Iran, governmental and religious pressures against women increased more and more until the revolution of Mahsa Amini began.

Those days were the peak of my and the people's efforts to save us from the corrupt government of the Islamic Republic.

The people in the cities of Iran rose up as one, young and old, with all their different strengths. They wanted freedom and a change of government.

We Iranian women want to live freely and to be given the respect we deserve.

We want to decide for ourselves to get a passport and leave our country, without needing the permission of our husband and father.

We want an optional hijab.

We want to have no political prisoners and certainly no execution of political prisoners.

We are against child marriage.

We are against fathers raping children or babies.

We want everyone in the community to have their rightful, respected place.

We want the right for women to hold a motorcycle license and to ride a bicycle.

We want freedom of expression.

We want equal rights.

The lonely road was school to me
by Hana

The roads of my life taught me it's okay to be scared. It's fine if I stumble, if I fall. I need to rise again, no matter how many times I am hit hard, I need to get back up each and every time to give it another try.

مشکلیں کتنی بھی ہوں ، زندگی میں چلتے جانا ہے ۔
یہ سفر ہمیشہ نبھا نا ہے۔

No matter how difficult this road is, I must carry on, and never stop. But I'm scared, I need to think which road is right to follow. Is it my left side? Right side? I need to see, to not be strangled and fall into a trap of deep darkness and pain. I am confused.

But wait - what is this voice? Where is it coming from? Why does it seem so kind and yet so strange? My heart says I should follow this road. I should listen to these whispers.

آو آگے بڑھو ،
میں تمہارے ساتھ ہوں ۔

And I heard some familiar words, "May this road lead you to a more dignified future, may this road and path give light to your wisdom and thoughts. And may you lead your own journey in your own way and may the sun shine bright upon your face and soul.

May you follow the road of never-ending happiness."

Amin.

Hope, Where are You?
by Besara

Among the people lost in the darkness
I heard that you were looking for me.

Yes, Hope. I have been looking for you for a long time
and believe me, what I am experiencing is very difficult.

They told me that boredom has taken hold of you.

Yes, Hope. My legs are cut off, my soul is dead,
but when I think of you, it seems like I have a cure.

Then ask me as many times as you want
and I will come to you.

The six words story
by all the group

I was
  looking at
      the sky
    the road
    stretches
        to a far
    destination
  I am ready
      for
something
  every day
    trying
      to fill
         the dark field
           of life
          with colourful
            flowers
             the skies
             flow
              with blue
            and green
             the weather
               of our hearts
              is not
             good

                        distance is
                    not always
                    a loss
                    life is
                  the journey
              of seeking
              knowledge
                if today
                can be
                  like this
                      it means
                            life
                              can bring us
                              joy
                                after the story
                        another story
                          under one inspiration
                          another inspiration
                    opened a new path
              while
            listening
          learning
      and sharing
    happily
      the liberation of
              heart
                  acceptance of
                  what you

cannot
change
never
alone
always
with
sad
books
I find
love
full
of sorrows
pity
regrets
better
remain
single
mind
says
hold on
heart
says
move on
I am
the moon
strong in
the darkness
all the dreams

blown
away
scorched
by
the fire
after
a busy
era
enjoy
freedom
happily
rise
shine
fall
and
rise
again
desperate
woman
searching
for
love
I am
the sky
the sun

The Hill
by Theja

You would see me and find me imposing,
someone who disturbs your scene:
an unapproachable fairy world, with folk of green trees, and bushes.
Silver-coloured waterfalls look from a distance like my loose hair.
Do you see I touch the sky? Clouds kiss my head.
You think I'm special, one who can do lots of things that you can't.

Don't look at me from afar. Start your journey to the top of the hill.
Slowly — step by step — carefully!
You can enjoy the beauty of the journey as long as you don't feel tired.
There are small rocks where you can sit and relax for a while, and small water springs to heal yourself.
They are not even a bit dirty.

When you reach the top, little by little, you will see the place you were before, from afar. How small it is.
At the end of the journey, the vast world unfolding
in front of your eyes can make you forget to breathe.
Even if you can't touch the clouds, swirling mist wraps around you,

but the sky is still distant.

So — think.
I am a part of this earth,
not a wonderful thing, out of reach.
Not an impossible goal for you to overcome.
You would feel the joy of victory
and your heart would be filled with pride.

Take a deep breath and enjoy the pleasure of the moment.
Express your happiness to the world lying beneath your feet.
When you go back, leave only your footprints
and take only the memories absorbed by your eyes and heart.
I am a hill, a part of nature just like you,
breaking the monotony of the earth and making this world colourful.

Reflections
by Alaa

When proximity hurts, then go away.

Distance isn't anger, but the space you leave for your heart

so that you do not suffer more.

Stay away no matter what your light is.

The lamp that gives the butterfly a light burns it if it gets too close.

And the sea quenches what is around. It will drown you if you go deep into it.

Distance is not always a loss.

A safe distance is how you take care of yourself.

and it brings you back to drawing clear lines of "love" for relatives and friends.

For all relationships, a safe distance restores your heart's balance.

And for your soul, peace be upon you.

Looking for
by Virginia

I would like to know
who I am.
Who I am beyond my traumas,
beyond my roles.

I would like to know who I am beyond my beliefs.
More than skin… conscience.
More than sin… virtues.
More than a body… spirit.

But
I still haven't found what I'm looking for.

An adolescent love story
by Stacy

I met him when I was 15 years old.
He was years too young to fall in love but we did.

I remember our first night together at a birthday party. He stayed the night.
In the morning he took me to his house for the first time.

Reaching there we fell asleep, as we were tired.
His mum found us in his room: "Wake up!"

He simply said to his mom, "She is your daughter-in-law."
It all started here.

We became too close, too in love.
We shared a lot of beautiful moments.

We grew up together. We stayed together.
I thought it would last for an eternity –

his wife, mother of his child. What a fairy tale!
Months passed and we started fighting,

arguing for any reason, lying and cheating.
We broke up, and started again and again.

Our love became such a mess.
But still our love for each other was strong.

We were young and both of us were searching for our way.
We were in love and we kept making mistakes.

After all the fights, all the chances, we broke up.
We were definitely finished.

This relationship had been too toxic.
Now I can't say that I hate him for not being there,

for not being the man I wanted him to be for me.
We were young and in love and we made mistakes.

But some mistakes can't be repaired.
He had been the first love of my life,

and though we are not together,
he will stay the first love in my heart.

I can't hate that love. I have tried but when I look back,
I realised that you can't hate pure love – an adolescent love story.
My past helped me to build my present and it made me who I am today.
I will always have good memories of my adolescent love.

Memories
by Theja

While lying alone on the bed on a cold winter night
my intolerable thoughts wander the past…

Somewhere far away on a sweaty summer night
to find cool relief we lie on a mat on the floor.

Two of us, with the most precious gifts in our lives.

Beyond the large glass door that separates us from the balcony,
I see the reflections of trees standing against a sky
filled with glittering stars.
Mango bunches swing in the occasional breeze,
touching the wall and making a soft sound.
A bat comes to find his food, is disturbed by the wind
and flies away. It breaks the silence of the night for a moment.

The Sepalika bush next to the mango tree is always full of flowers.
They wake up and bloom at night.
They waft through the panels and we breathe them in.

Our bodies slowly cool down.
Little ones sleepily roll closer and seek warmth from us.

The cold we felt is slowly decreasing. Warmth fills our hearts
and I realise this is the love and bond of a family.

I still remember the scent of Sepalika flowers.
I still hear a flying bat, the chatter of an owl,
and though the three of you are no longer beside me
to share the sweetness of dark nights,
I feel these memories, always with me.

The Most Beautiful Memories of Childhood
by Besara

My parents woke up first.

> Good morning, our little daughter —
> how was your sleep?

Good morning Mom and Dad, I slept very well.

> Our little ones — get up, eat breakfast.
> It is a beautiful day
> and we will learn to ride bicycles.

Bicycles? We don't have bicycles.

> We have a surprise for you —
> for today is an important day.

Thank you, I love you very much.
I want to play with the bike right away —
I don't want an ordinary morning!

> Our little one, you must eat breakfast
> to be able to play.

This is why, without desire I ate breakfast.
Then my mom, dad, two brothers, my sister and I

all went out together to learn to ride a bike
and they were happy to see me learn.

Breakfasts, lunches, dinners with my family
are the most beautiful memories of my life.

The Distant Hills
by Alaa

The wide meadows,
the cotton clouds,

the wooden gate at the entrance
to the beautiful field.

I imagine them.
All the things that are gone.

I imagine the war has not taken everything,
and will not stay.

A Mother
by Virginia

A mother cries for her son in other lands,
a mother survives on memories,
a mother hopes for life
and lives in hope
of her son in her arms again.
A mother prays for her son –
roof over his head, bread and water.
A mother gives comfort and food
and welcomes the unknown,
offers her kindness
so that God the Father extends his love
and reaches the son
who once was born in pain
and with pain has left to seek a new life.
Because his mother is worth
every sacrifice of freedom
and every sacrifice of love.
A mother cries for her son in other lands
and survives on calls,
photos and videos on her phone.

My Father
by Besara

My father. My soul hurts
in every word I write for you.
I don't want you to remain
the most beautiful, painful dream of my life.

I can't let you be just a memory,
I want you here with me.
I miss the melody of your voice,
your advice, your positivity.

I miss the beauty of your soul
expressed in your actions.
You were a beautiful man
with a beautiful world.

I lost your presence, Father,
because God wanted you by his side.
I shed tears, missing you, but
you are a thousand reasons to smile.

Celestial Chains: A journey through the Temple of Dreams
by Sachal

In the embrace of a summer night, where silence echoes like a pin drop, a gentle warmth caresses the air. Silver beams descend on the earth, casting a divine glow on the deserted streets as if the town itself has vanished. I find myself alone, traversing the empty streets, carrying not just bags of hopes but also the weight of the moment suspended in time. It feels as if celestial beings welcome me with every step.

As I climb the stairs of the old temple of dreams, each step is lit by a candle, casting a soft glow around me. The flickering light guides my way, creating a serene and enchanting atmosphere. The entrance door sparkles with tiny stars, like diamonds in the moonlight. The magical sight welcomes me to the ancient temple of dreams.

I walk through the door, and another staircase leads me down to the main hall. In the centre stands the fountain of tears. The tranquil sound of the flowing water echoes through the hall, adding to the peaceful atmosphere of the ancient temple.

The walls show my memories like a movie, each moment flickering like scenes from a favourite film. Looking up at the sky, I see myself as shiny stars lost in the vast expanse above.

Right by the fountain of tears, I find myself glowing in the dark sky.

I am lost in the sky, in a trance. When I close my eyes, peace fills my mind and I hear the message of my heartbeat in the darkness: deep breaths and flowing water. I feel like I am floating, embracing the serenity of the moment.

I am floating above the clouds, delving into the dark sky, hoping to touch the stars, hoping to find my lost self. As I get close to the stars, I wonder why I can't go further, longing to move ahead. Looking down I notice my feet chained. The chains from the sky connect to the hall's floor.

My eyes well up and my tears glow and cascade into the fountain of tears. Each tear transforms into balls of light that illuminate the fountain and hall from above.

A sorrowful sight unfolds as more tears fall, creating a moonlike reflection of the hall. I feel a sense of melancholy as I long to move forward but feel restrained by tears and chains.

Inertia
by Virginia

I am less than an atom
journeying for hours
I ceased to exist

I went from matter
to antimatter

whilst my body crossed
an ocean
an astral journey

nauseating ideas invade my head
what's going on
what's going on

times moves forward
while I
I become nothing

I was like a black ant on a black stone in a black night
by Falone

When I lose all hope,
when light stops coming in,

When the road stops,
and there is no direction to take,

When the rain stops falling,
and the water stops flowing,

Hope never leaves my heart,
even when hopeless.

Days never stop dawning,
days never stop changing,
days never stop flowing.

The days will continue until the end of our lives.

Better days are coming.

Dear Diary
by Besara

You have always been my friend
and listened to my confessions.
Every moment I've spent,
you have smiled and cried with me.
Each moment we've spent together
is engraved with a pen in my soul forever.
You allowed me to express myself
the way I really felt - the stories that I lived
and carry in my broken heart.
No one else can fully understand the way I feel.
Even when I make mistakes, you don't abandon me.
This is enough for me.
In the most difficult moments of my life,
you are here.

Poverty
by Alaa

It is wrong to think that poverty
is the poverty of pockets.
It is the poverty of hearts.

Empty pockets may be filled with money one day.
But empty hearts – they cannot be filled
with feelings and sensations.

How poor are those hearts that forgive and do not forgive.
I had no familiarity and comfort.
I was nothing but a garden whose leaves fell

and roses withered on my branches
and left me shamed.
I was empty on my throne.

Hearts that do not love others
and are not filled with love – even if
they are alive, they are dead.

What is Life?
by Besara

Many times we have asked, "Why did God put me in this difficulty?"
Why don't we understand that this is a precious life?
We have to make life worthwhile
even when we are in the midst of a storm, pain or destruction.
Let's walk the path of positivity.
It will certainly not be easy –
we will face many challenges
and from them we will learn our skills and courage,
our weakness and the strength of our faith.
So, to be on the right path, we must face obstacles.
They will come disguised and we will not understand
that they are blessed.
Many times we have asked, "Why did God put me in this difficulty?"
But after the rain comes the sun.

The global family
by Abu Rina

We came from everywhere, were called by the instinct to survive from all corners of the earth. Our pilgrimage was in the name of humanity and life, not to protect ideas or cultures but our existence.

We were pushed to flee from nothingness to take refuge in the embrace of the unknown.

Humanity, dignity and life deserve continuity and human values that protect us from evil, oppression and injustice must exist.

I could not imagine the coexistence of a global family was possible except in St Augustine's.

Thank you to those who made this idea possible. This centre made us accept all cultures, values and colours. It helped us create a new reality, a model of a peaceful world. It was an imagined and utopian world that became possible thanks to the values established by the St Augustine's Centre.

Once we entered the centre, everyone's barriers of fear melted away. Difference dissolved and our world became one family, a safe place for all. As the centre members, we represent the entire world because we come from many countries. Saint

Augustine's is the imagined and alternative world that we dreamed of and searched for.

Our moral responsibility is to spread the values of Saint Augustine's to all parts of the world so that it becomes a safe place for everyone. This small model deserves to be generalised; its values spread throughout the globe. Thank you to those who provided the means for life and protected the values of survival and coexistence.

I am a Tiny Bee
by Theja

I am not an animal or a bird. Not a colourful creature
but I colour the entire Earth with my skills.

I am a tiny insect, but I offer you
the most nutritious and sweetest thing in the world.

Listen to my sound — M… M… M… M…
Stand still for a minute and focus on it.

It is a sound of unity, of commitment, of cleverness, of creativity.

Look at my home. No! Our home. You won't believe your eyes —
how symmetrical every part of it is, the fruitful end of our perfect teamwork.

See how we communicate, how I dance, round and round,
how the others recognise what I say.

How far are the flower fields that I collected nectar from?
No hidden secrets. No competition. We fill our hive with honey.

We are loyal to our queen. If she is protected, so will all generations be.
We sacrifice our lives for them.

Do you ever see us fighting? We do our duty to our colony.
We enjoy it. We don't know laziness.

I never boast about what I do for the earth, but we save the vegetation,
all for you. Not for us.

If you hurt me, I would sting. No hard feelings. It's self-protection.
Did you know one sting would end my life? So please be kind.

Otherwise, I will have to choose death.

Do you know the biggest animal on the earth? The wild elephant —
but we can control him, with our power of unity.

Nature is always kind to me but you are between us,
though we both are parts of it. I never want to change it.
Please don't change it.

A home to the homeless
by Falone

We are immigrants.
We come from different countries for security, peace and protection.
We are not agents of disorder.

We are not here because we wanted to be,
but because life and destiny chose to bring us here.
For us, England is a welcoming and kind land,
giving a second chance to our lives.

Just like a mother who protects all her children,
this country has given us a chance to smile again,
and a glimmer of hope for the future.

Be blessed! Welcoming land, hope-giver for the hopeless,
comforter of our sorrows, you will remain the land that freed me.
Despite all past difficulties, you give us solace.

Thanks, England, for responding to our pain.
We have come to weep at your feet, children from every nation.
You received us. You listened to our cries and decided to intervene.

Thank you for giving us a home.
Thank you for giving us food.
Thank you for giving us hope for a better future.
Thank you for being there for us.

Long life to you England.
Long life to the people of England.
Long life to the King of England.
Long life to the Prime Minister.
Long life to all the communities that stand up for us.

We love you and will be eternally grateful.
I use the voice of all immigrants to say thanks.
Be blessed, England.

The Writer's Refuge Allowed Me
by Anise

To expand my horizons,
to experience not only through my own eyes
but through the perspectives of others
from worlds different from mine.

It taught me how to capture scents, colours
and emotions, how to put into words
things that are hard to even imagine.
It taught me that writing is more
than telling stories,
it's about taking details
and crafting a complex world
within the words.

A Walk in Halifax with my Mother
by Besara

Mom, I saw Halifax town today.

> Tell me my daughter —
> I'm curious now.

Mama, Halifax is a cradle of cultural and natural heritage.

> I like how you started this description, you reminded me of your dad.
> You look so much like him.

Mom, I love you both — him in Heaven, and you so far away.

> But what did Halifax offer us?
> Tell me, I will listen carefully.

Thanks Mom. We started with a light walk, to enjoy the trees and flowers that surrounded us. We often stopped, exploring the natural beauty beyond the historical and cultural wonders. There were adventures for those who wanted them, and nature provided us with a relaxing picnic setting: a quiet contrast to the energy of the city. Everyone chose what they liked from the menu.

After the break, I continued exploring, and with every step, in my mind I noted —
1.	Halifax has enviable cultural values, inherited from history.
2.	In preserving its culture, Halifax also looks forward to the development
of tourism.
3.	Thanks to its favourable geographical position and its harmonious weave,
it has a positive energy.
4.	The heart of Halifax a very special look because of its architecture.
5.	The preservation of the past by future generations was evident, and as I walked, I felt respect for the generations that have preserved this extraordinary town.

These are some of the images that will remain deeply etched in my memory.

> Oh, my daughter, I am very happy too.
> I'm sorry that I couldn't hold back the tears
> but you made me so happy
> that for a moment it seemed as if I was there with you.

My name is not asylum seeker
by Abu Rina

I am a tree whose roots have been torn from home soil
who wants to be planted in a new earth.

This new soil is the community of Halifax,
My roots are the people of Halifax.

The connections give me love, a sense of belonging.
I am a love and life seeker.

I am a fish who was hooked from the water,
I am the one who searched for another planet.

I feel alive and safe, permitted.
I am a new world seeker.

End of a Happy Journey
by Theja

I came out like a water bubble from the dark womb of the earth.
Look at the blue sky and shady greens. How beautiful this world is!
But I can't stay here. Now I begin my journey with hope.
There will be more beautiful, and perhaps ugly things ahead.

The blue sky fades and the darkness of rain is visible.
But a rainbow quenches my heart. Ah! Here are raindrops.
Now I understand, they feed me.
There is beauty in something that is bad at first glance.

I flow slowly while learning nature.
The trees on both sides bend inwards, like they are kissing me.
Their shadows apply make-up on my surface.
Colourful birds in their arms talk to each other, like a soothing
piece of music.

The sun rays create glamorous patterns, but are oppressive at noon.
No worries. Trees make shade and look after me.

Who is sneak-peeking around me? Tiny fish! There are big, aggressive ones too,
    and I hide the little ones among my waves to protect them
    as much as possible.

Now I am stronger. Ah! Who is here now? Human beings.
They can use me in both good and bad ways. Decide my survival.
Some people hurt me. Destroy my green friends, crack my banks.
I am helpless now. When the time comes, I will teach them a lesson.

    Rain! Are you helping me?
    They must understand that if they are kind to me,
    I will offer my kindness to them.
    If I am protected, they will be protected too.

    I have come many miles, a long way. I fulfilled my duty
        to this amazing world and I am tired. Now I need a place to rest.
    Here's my destination, waiting for me. The great ocean!
    I can hear, I can see, I can feel, the waves are forming and breaking.

    Yes! In a little while I will hide in your arms.

I am called happiness
by Hana

I am here to cuddle you
I am here standing tall,
high like lush green trees to give shade when you're tired.
میں گھنا سایہ دار درخت ہوں ، جب تم زمانے کی تھکان سے چور ہو جاؤ تو چلے آنا ۔

I am a friend like these winds,
you may share your happiness with me.

I am your unspoken words, your untold truth, I am your friend.
I am your never-ending promise,
I am when and how you make me or shape me,
I am that water, I can quench your soul.
میں تم میں اور تم مجھ سے ہو۔

I am Me and I am You
I am the night, waiting for sunrise.

The goodness of the heart
by Falone

Always choose to be good.

Goodness makes life beautiful,
goodness makes life longer,
goodness gives colour to life.

Always choose to be good.

The fruit of goodness never fails.
Goodness is the friend who keeps you happy
when other friends are gone.

Always choose to be good.

When people see only bad in your actions,
always choose to be good.

When people reject you,
always choose to be good.

Make tomorrow better with your soul.

I'm here to stay
by Sachal

Just break your cuffs,
Come rise above.
Just beat that fear,
Come rise above.

Come pray the Lord,
Let faith erupt!
We're brave enough
To shake the world.

I'm blessed enough,
I'll rise and twirl.
No stress, no grief,
I've trained enough.

A whole new soul,
Calm and cool enough.
Riding the waves,
I'm strong enough.

In this vibrant life
I'm finding my way,
I'm here to stay,
I'm here to stay…

I Am Anise
by Anise

I am Anise. I rose from Iran, a land whose wounds still run deep within me, a girl whose only dream was freedom and equality. The walls of prison surrounded me, but my will was a root pushing through stone. The night taught me that darkness is not an end but a beginning.

When my world crumbled, I crossed borders soaked in blood and lands drowning in death and despair. I walked through storms and forests and marshes, each step heavier than the last. I ate leaves and drank swamp water. Survival was my only choice. On the journey, I sacrificed everything I had to stay alive.

With each border I crossed, a new flame ignited within me, a fire no cruelty could extinguish. I knew the price of freedom was suffering, but that pain led me to a brighter tomorrow.

I arrived in a land unfamiliar to me, but for a soul forged in hardship no place is truly foreign. Empty-handed but full of faith, I am building a new future.

I am no longer the girl in the ruins – I have risen from my ashes. I stand here to create a space of kindness and hope for others. I am Anise. I hope that one day my name will remain as someone who fought for a better world, who stood against injustice and fought for freedom.

World in one centre
by Abu Rina

Oh, what a miracle!
Paradise on earth!
One size fits all –
take a seat in that hall.
Play piano, scrabble and football.
Let's go climb the hills and visit The Piece Hall.

Hills
by Hana

You can climb anytime, anywhere
I'll be your refuge.
Meet me at the top where the green grass grows,
Where the birds have flown up and gone.
Come and take rest, feel the fresh air and embrace it through your soul and breath.
I want you to spend the night with me and count the stars, share your story starting with tears, ending with laughter.
See how silent the trees are, their journey and poetry of their inner being.
Standing tall and alone at the times of storms and darkness, only mountains and hills all around.

اِسنو ، سنو
، زندگی کی جھنکار
، ہوا کا سنگھار
اور میری روح کی پکار ۔

Listen. Listen.........!!!
'The Songs the Earth Writes, the Music of my Soul.
The Whispers of my Heart.'

Hope and Freedom
by Hana

She was living like a caged bird within her house,
but when she finally wanted to reach the sky,
she had already forgotten how to fly.
She finally learnt to grow, glow and self love.
، تو میرا حوصلہ دیکھ ، داد تو دے کہ اب مجھے شوق کمال بھی نہیں
خوف زوال بھی نہیں ۔
Look at my hope and strength, give me a pat on my shoulder.
I finally have no fear of falling!

Live With It
by Anise

Never be ashamed of anything in your life.
Every scar,
every mistake,
every victory,
every failure.
They're all part of the story that made you who you are.

Live with it.
Embrace it.

When I Am Old
by Abu Rina

I will tell the world what has not been told.
I will be more independent; I will be bold.
I will follow a diet, eat food without salt.
I will eat fruit and drink juice instead of wine.
When it gets dark, I will see better and my face will shine.
I will rebuild my life, I will retire from work and social life.
I will receive no calls. If you text me, that's fine.
I will feel the pain in my knees and spine, but I'll tell my doctor all is fine.
I will talk with myself and the books on my shelf.
I will stop time, I will not die, I am serious, no lie.
When I cut across you, I don't say hi.
I will wear large clothes, let my trousers fall down, I won't tie.
I will talk alone and laugh, I'm not shy.
When I meet a friend in a café, I leave him alone, don't say bye.
When I grow old, I will tell the world what has not been told.